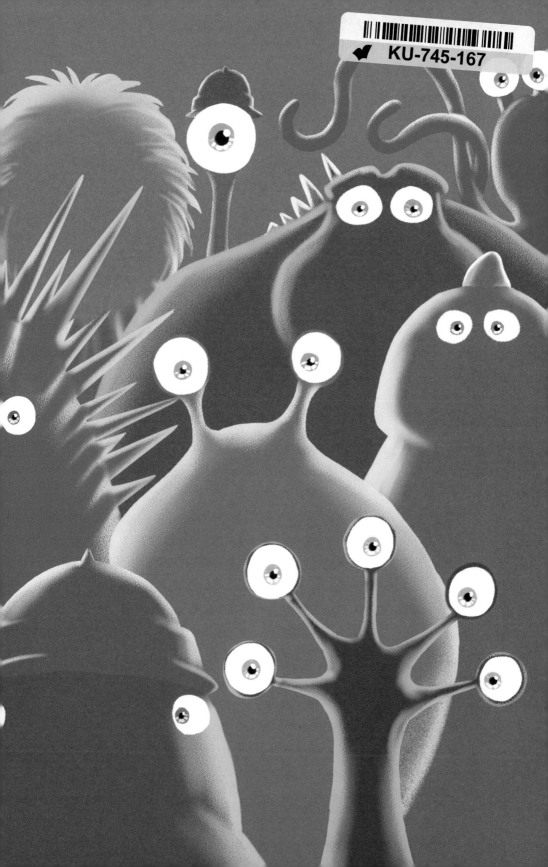

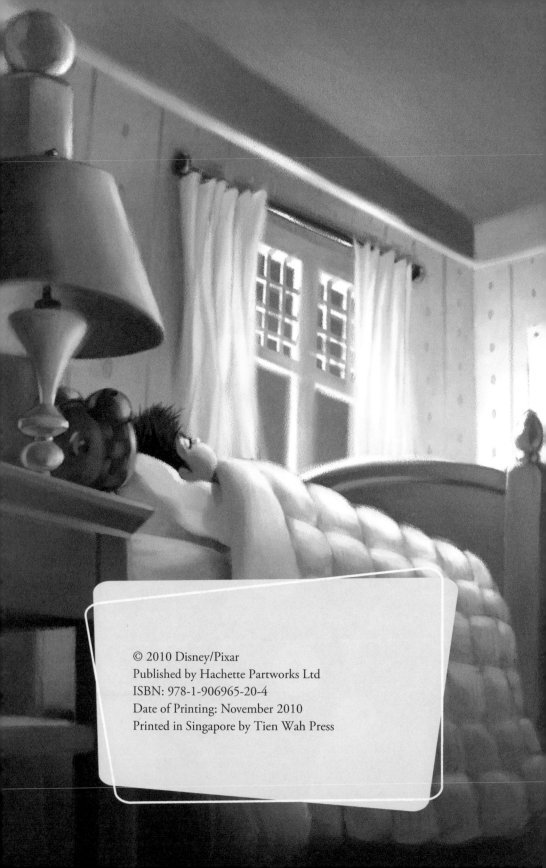

Published by Hachette Partworks Ltd
ISBN: 978-1-906965-20-4
Date of Printing: November 2010
Printed in Singapore by Tien Wah Press

DISNEY·PIXAR

MONSTERS, INC.

DISNEY·PIXAR

hachette

All children know that there are monsters in their bedrooms. And at night, those monsters will come out and scare them.

What children *don't* know is that the monsters are just doing their jobs. Monsters need to scare children and collect their screams. The monsters then turn their screams into electricity for the city of Monstropolis, where the monsters live.

Early one morning, a furry blue monster named Sulley and his best friend, Mike, were walking to work at Monsters, Inc. Sulley was the top Scarer at Monsters, Inc., and Mike was his assistant.

Mike and Sulley stopped in the lobby of Monsters, Inc.
"Happy birthday," Mike said to his girlfriend, Celia.
"Oh, Googly-Woogly, you remembered!" Celia said
happily.

Mike was taking her out to dinner that evening, and
she knew he had picked a great restaurant.

Then Sulley and Mike went up to the workers' locker room to get ready for work. All of a sudden a monster named Randall appeared out of nowhere!

"AAHH!" shouted a surprised Mike.

Randall could make himself invisible by blending into any background. But he was jealous of Sulley. Randall wanted to be the top Scarer at Monsters, Inc.

Mike and Sulley went to the Scare Floor. There, lots of monsters had gathered in front of a long row of doors. These were the doors that let the monsters into the bedrooms of children in the human world.

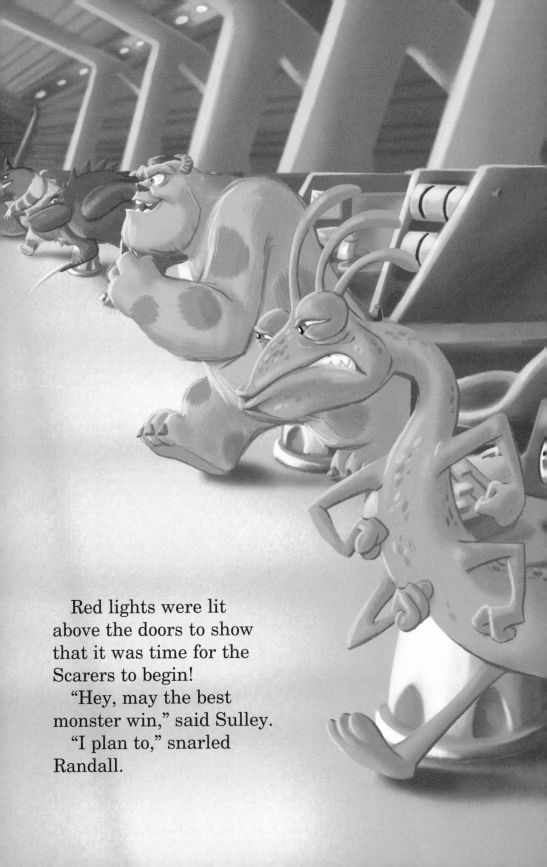

Red lights were lit
above the doors to show
that it was time for the
Scarers to begin!

"Hey, may the best
monster win," said Sulley.

"I plan to," snarled
Randall.

Randall quickly scared a lot of kids – and collected a lot of screams. His assistant, Fungus, proudly pointed at the scoreboard. Randall was winning!

But then Sulley scared all the children at a slumber party! Sulley was still the top Scarer at Monsters, Inc.

Suddenly someone shouted, "Twenty-three-nineteen! We have a twenty-three-nineteen!" A child's sock had been spotted on the back of a monster named George.

Special agents from the Child Detection Agency – the CDA – had to come to decontaminate George. After all, every monster knows that children and their things are toxic!

Soon the workday was over. Just as Mike was
about to leave with Celia, Roz stopped him. Roz was
in charge of paperwork. Mike had forgotten to hand
in his scare reports again.

Sulley told Mike that he would take care of the
paperwork. So, while Mike left with Celia, Sulley
headed back to the Scare Floor.

Sulley thought the Scare Floor
was empty – until a little girl
grabbed his tail! He was terrified!
After all, kids were even more
toxic than their socks! Panicking,
Sulley tried to find the right
door so he could put the little
girl back in her room.

But the little girl wasn't scared of Sulley at all.
"Kitty," she called to him. She wanted to play!
Sulley finally managed to put her into a duffel bag.
But just then he spotted Randall. Sulley quickly hid.
He couldn't let anyone find out about this!

Sulley didn't know what to do. So he went to
find Mike.

Mike wasn't happy about having his romantic
dinner with Celia interrupted. And he was
terrified when the little girl crept out of the bag.
He wasn't the only one who was scared. Monsters
everywhere screamed.

Mike and Sulley managed to whisk the girl
away before CDA agents arrived at the restaurant.

No-one saw Mike and Sulley take the child home. But helicopters had begun to search the city for her. Mike and Sulley tried to come up with a plan to get her back to her own bedroom.

In the meantime, they needed to keep her happy – but not too happy. Whenever the little girl laughed, she caused a power surge that lit up all the lights. If that kept happening, it would be easy for the CDA agents to find her.

Eventually, the girl fell asleep. By now, Sulley was actually growing fond of her. Perhaps children weren't dangerous after all. Mike, however, wasn't so sure.

The next morning, they disguised her as a little monster and brought her back to Monsters, Inc. The trio had to walk right past their boss, Mr. Waternoose, while he was talking to a CDA agent.

  While Mike went to find the key to the girl's door,
Sulley began to play hide-and-seek with her. He
even gave her a nickname – Boo.
  "What are you doing?" Mike asked Sulley when he
entered the room.
  "Uh... I'm looking for the kid," answered Sulley.
  "You lost it?" asked Mike in disbelief.
  Suddenly Boo ran and jumped into Sulley's arms.

Just then they heard a noise. It was Randall and Fungus. The trio quickly hid. Fungus held a newspaper. "It's on the front page!" he said. "The child! The one you were after!"

Randall told Fungus to act as if nothing had happened and to take care of the "machine". Randall would deal with the monster who had let the kid into Monstropolis.

Randall was up to something. But what?

But Mike and Sulley had more important things on their minds. They managed to sneak Boo up to the Scare Floor so that they could put her back in her bedroom.

Sulley was getting ready to say goodbye when he told Mike to wait. He didn't have the right door.

"What are you talking about? Of course it's her door!" insisted Mike. While they were arguing, Boo wandered off.

Unfortunately, as Sulley and Mike searched for Boo, they ran straight into Randall.

"So what do you think of that kid getting out, Sullivan? Pretty crazy, huh?" Randall said.

"Oh, yeah," Sulley said slowly. "Crazy. Heh-heh."

Then Celia appeared. "Last night was one of the worst nights of my entire life!" she shouted at Mike.

Randall listened in. Looking at his newspaper closely, he spotted Mike in the picture taken at the restaurant where the kid had been seen. Suddenly Randall realised that Mike and Sulley had the kid!

Mike could see what was coming, so he tried to run away. But Randall soon caught up with him.

"Where's the kid?" Randall demanded.

"I don't know," Mike sputtered. But Randall didn't believe him. Randall told Mike that he'd have the kid's door on the Scare Floor during lunch. But Mike had to make sure the girl was there so they could get her back to the human world.

Meanwhile, Sulley was still searching for Boo. He rounded a corner and saw her fall into a rubbish bin. "No!" he shouted as two monsters wheeled the bin up to a compactor.

By the time Sulley reached the compactor room, everything but one eyestalk had been crushed into a tiny cube. Sulley was heartbroken.

Mike caught up with his friend. "Sulley! Great news, buddy! I got us a way out of this mess, but we gotta hurry. Where is...?"

But before Mike could finish, they heard the sound of Boo's voice. She hadn't been crushed after all! Sulley hugged Boo tightly.

Mike, Sulley and Boo hurried back to the Scare Floor. Boo's door was in Randall's station, just as Randall had promised.

But Sulley came to a sudden halt. Randall! They couldn't trust Randall. He was after Boo!

Mike was sure that everything was safe. To prove it, he entered Boo's room. Just then a box snapped closed over Mike. It was a trap!

Sulley and Boo hid. They watched Randall wheel the box away.

Sulley had to help his pal! He also needed to see what Randall was up to. So he and Boo followed Randall.

Luckily, Boo discovered a secret passageway.

At the end of the passageway, they found Randall's secret lab. In it, he had a machine that could suck the screams out of a child. But now it was Mike who was strapped to the machine!

Randall was furious. He wanted to know where the little girl was. Of course, Mike wouldn't tell him.

Just then Sulley pulled out the machine's plug. And he, Boo and Mike managed to get away.

The three friends raced down the hall. Mike was
desperate to escape, but Sulley had another idea.
He decided to go to Mr. Waternoose for help. Mike
told him about Randall's evil plan.

To their surprise, Waternoose picked up Boo.
Then he pushed Sulley and Mike out through a
huge metal door into the human world. They
were banished!

Mike was furious. "Oh, what a great idea!" he shouted at Sulley. "Going to your old pal Waternoose! Too bad he was in on the whole thing!"

But Sulley could think only of saving Boo. He knew they couldn't go back the way they had come.

Suddenly a giant shadow covered the ground. They looked up to see the Yeti, the Abominable Snowman.

The Yeti told Sulley that there was a village nearby. This gave Sulley an idea. If he found a child's bedroom, it might lead him back to Monstropolis. Quickly he built a sleigh from supplies in the Yeti's cave and set off.

Mike was angry with Sulley, so Mike stayed behind.

In no time, Sulley found a child's bedroom and was back at Monsters, Inc. He raced down the passageway that led to Randall's secret lab. Suddenly Sulley heard Boo's frightened voice close by.

"Boo! I'm here! Where are you?" whispered Sulley.

Sulley found Boo strapped to the scream machine. He smashed the machine and rescued Boo. The machine crashed into Waternoose and Fungus, pinning them to the wall.

"Stop wasting time! Finish him off!" Waternoose shouted to Randall, as Sulley and Boo escaped.

Sulley and an invisible Randall
fought furiously over Boo. In
the middle of the fight, Mike
came back – just in time to hit
Randall with a snowball! This
allowed Sulley to escape down the
hallway with Mike and Boo.

The trio reached the Scare Floor with Randall right behind them. Then Sulley had an idea. They raced up to the moving doorways. Sulley told Mike to make Boo laugh. As Boo laughed, all the red door lights lit up. Sulley, Mike and Boo jumped back and forth through different doors, hoping to lose Randall.

But Randall finally caught Boo and fled. Sulley followed him and found Boo alone. When Sulley ran to her, Randall attacked. Boo was afraid, but she had to help! So she grabbed Randall's hair and pulled.

That was all Sulley needed. He threw Randall through another door that led into the human world – never to be heard from again.

Back on the Scare Floor, Mr. Waternoose and
a group of CDA agents were waiting for them.
Suddenly Mike had an idea – he took Boo's costume
and ran as fast as he could. The agents, believing
the costume to be Boo, began chasing Mike. In the
commotion, Sulley and Boo managed to get away.

Mr. Waternoose finally caught up with Sulley and Boo. In his anger, he told them that the city of Monstropolis didn't have enough energy. So they had to find an alternative to scaring. He wanted to kidnap kids from the human world and extract their screams with the machine. That was why Randall had been looking for Boo!

"I'll kidnap a thousand children before I let this company die!" Mr. Waternoose vowed.

But Roz, who turned out to be the CDA boss, heard his confession. Mr. Waternoose was taken away by CDA agents.

Finally, it was time to send Boo home. Sulley
took Boo back to her room and tucked the little
girl into bed.

"Nothing's coming to scare you any more.
Right?" he said. Boo smiled. "Goodbye, Boo," he
whispered. Slowly, Sulley crossed to the door. He
looked back at Boo, who watched him from the
bed. Quietly, Sulley closed the door behind him.

Back in the Scare Room, two CDA agents moved in. They shredded Boo's door and took it away. Sadly Sulley picked up a small piece of the door. At least he had this to remind him of Boo.

Mike knew how much Sulley already missed Boo. "Come on, pal, cheer up!" he said, as they left Monsters, Inc. "We got Boo home! Sure, we're both out of a job... but hey, at least we had some laughs."

Sulley smiled. Mike had just given him an idea!

Time passed, and Sulley turned the Scream Floor into a Laugh Floor. Now, monsters made kids laugh instead of scream to generate electricity. Boo had showed them that laughter was ten times as powerful as screams. The energy crisis was over in Monstropolis!

Still, Sulley missed his little friend Boo. So one day, Mike glued her entire door back together. That way, Sulley could visit Boo whenever he liked! And that's just what he did!